Josiah Gilbert Holland

The Puritan's Guest

And other Poems

Josiah Gilbert Holland

The Puritan's Guest
And other Poems

ISBN/EAN: 9783744772129

Printed in Europe, USA, Canada, Australia, Japan

Cover: Foto ©Andreas Hilbeck / pixelio.de

More available books at **www.hansebooks.com**

THE PURITAN'S GUEST

AND OTHER POEMS

DR. J. G. HOLLAND'S WRITINGS.

Complete Works. 16 Volumes. Small 12mo.
Sold separately.

Complete Sets, 16 vols., *in a box;* half calf, $44.00; half morocco, gilt top, $46.00; and cloth, $20.00.

Illustrated Edition, 14 vols., 12mo, cloth. New style. Sold only in sets, $20.00.

COMPLETE POETICAL WRITINGS.

With illustrations by Reinhart, Griswold, and Mary Hallock Foote, and a portrait by Wyatt Eaton. 8vo, $3.50.

Holiday Edition of the same.

In extra cloth, full gilt sides and edges, . . . $5.00

THE PURITAN'S GUEST

AND OTHER POEMS

BY

J. G. HOLLAND

NEW YORK
CHARLES SCRIBNER'S SONS
1891

TROW'S
PRINTING AND BOOKBINDING COMPANY
201–213 *East Twelfth Street*
NEW YORK

CONTENTS.

Contents.

THE PURITAN'S GUEST

THE PURITAN'S GUEST.

I.

THE house stood back from the old Bay Road
   That wound through Sudbury town;
Before it a brawling streamlet flowed;
   Behind it the woods shut down.

Dwelt there the Puritan, good John Guye,
   With the daughters God had given,—
Three beautiful maidens fair and shy,
   Whose mother was in heaven.

And one was Patience, so tall and fair;
  And one was queenly Prue;
And one was Hope with the golden hair;
  And the eyes of all were blue.

And horsemen, riding along that way,
  Drank at the household spring,
And asked of the maids the time. o' day,
  Or brought them news of the King.

It seemed like a glimpse of heaven to see,
  In sun and storm the same,
These three fair maidens at windows three
  To the riders who went and came.

It seemed like an hour in heaven to sit,
  When the winter wind blew hoarse,
And watch these diligent maidens knit,
  And hear John Guye's discourse.

If love was lighted, ah, who may say!—

It was centuries ago;—

And maids were the same in the olden day

That they are now, I trow.

. And who shall wonder, or who condemn—

For their life had scanty zest—

*If dangerous fancies came to them,

As the men rode east and west?

Guye ruled his house by the olden law,

And he knew the heart of a maid;

And, watching with godly care, he saw

What made his soul afraid!

For smiles shone up from the saucy lips

That drank at the household spring,

And kisses were tossed from finger-tips

With the tidings of the King.

And the eyes that should have flamed with fire,
  And spurned these gallant arts,
Grew soft and sad with a strange desire,
  Over tender and troubled hearts.

"Ah God!" groaned the Puritan, good John Guye,
  "That such a woe can be!—
That their mother should be in heaven, and I
  Should be left with daughters three!"

(And one was Patience, so tall and fair;
  And one was queenly Prue;
And one was Hope with the golden hair;
  And the eyes of all were blue.)

II.

From the bitter sea it had blown all day,
  And the night came hurrying down;
And snow from a sky all cold and gray
  Was whitening Sudbury town.

The chimney roared like an angry beast,

   With eyes and tongues of fire,

And the crazy windows facing east

   Shook in the tempest's ire.

The sleety snow fell heavy and fast;

   It beat on the roof like rain;

And the forest hurtled beneath the blast

   Of the dreadful hurricane!

The autumn leaves that had flown all day,

   In wild and scurrying flocks,

Were pelted down by the hail, and lay

   Huddled among the rocks.

" 'Tis a fearful storm!" said good John Guye,

   As he looked at his daughters three;

" And the riders abroad to-night must die;

   And many such there be!"

Their cheeks grew pale in the ruddy blaze
  With what their ears had heard,
And they looked in the fire with grieved amaze;
  But they could not speak a word.

(And one was Patience, so tall and fair;
  And one was queenly Prue;
And one was Hope with the golden hair;
  And the eyes of all were blue.)

'Twas an owl flew hooting out of the trees,
  In a lull of the tempest's wrath;
And caught mid-air by the crafty breeze,
  He wrestled for his path.

He wrestled long, but he strove in vain
  With the fierce and blinding gloom;
He was shot like a bolt through the window-pane,
  And a great gust filled the room.

They sprang to their feet in sharp affright,
    But still no word they said,
As they stopped the window from the night;
    And the great white bird lay dead!

" 'Tis a fearful storm!" said good John Guye;
    " Heaven help all those abroad!
For the men who ride, and the birds that fly,
    Let us kneel and pray to God!"

But while they knelt, and the hoary saint
    Groaned with the stress of prayer,
They heard from a wanderer, far and faint,
    A shriek of wild despair.

" Thank God!" said the Puritan, rising straight;
    " Thank God, my daughters three,
That the answer of heaven does not wait,
    And my guest has come to me!"

He flung to the wall the oaken door;

   He passed it with a bound;

And plunging into the darkness frore,

   He listened along the ground.

Prone on the path he found his guest;

   His hair was streaming wild;

Guye lifted him to his mighty breast

   As he had been a child.

The maidens three peered into the storm;

   It smote their brows like death;

They saw their father's stalwart form;

   They heard his struggling breath.

(And one was Patience, so tall and fair;

   And one was queenly Prue;

And one was Hope with the golden hair;

   And the eyes of all were blue.)

They laid the stranger before the flame,

    They nursed him till he stirred,—

Till he opened his eyes, and spoke a name!—

    'Twas a woman's name they heard!

They nursed him long with tender care,

    The while he moaned and wept;

He wakened anon to breathe a prayer

    And anon he sank and slept.

The ghostly shade of a man he seemed;

    His teeth were white as milk;

And the long white curls on his forehead gleamed

    Like skeins of tangled silk.

His eyes peered out with an eerie stare,—

    They were wondrous deep and large,—

And they looked like mountain tarns aglare

    Beneath their beetling marge!

He rose straight up from his lowly bed;
  He looked at the maidens three;
" I have lost my wits, you see," he said;
  " I have lost my wits," said he.

Each maid bowed low as he gazed at her,
  In the sweet, old-fashioned way;
For they guessed that he was a minister
  From the Massachusetts Bay.

(And one was Patience, so tall and fair;
  And one was queenly Prue;
And one was Hope with the golden hair;
  And the eyes of all were blue.)

He looked above and he looked around;
  With fear their bosoms beat;
He looked till the lifeless bird he found,
  And he lifted it by its feet.

He lifted it in his tender hands;
  He nursed it on his breast;
" Oh God!" he groaned, "in what strange lands
  Does my own dear birdling rest!"

He sang to the bird a thin, old tune;
  It quavered like a rill
That, leaping the leafy steps of June,
  Goes purling at its will.

He smoothed the feathers upon its neck
  With his fingers pale and fine :
" She was white as thee, thou snowy wreck,
  But her fate is worse than thine!"

And then he wept like a silly child,
  And the maidens wept around;
For they doubted his wits had wandered wild
  And his heart had a cruel wound.

" Prythee tell thy tale "—the voice was Guye's—

   " If thou hast tale to tell ; "

The Puritan brushed his blinded eyes,

   And the maidens hearkened well.

They leaned to list to the tale accursed ;

   He leaned to their eyes, and said :

" I think, 'twas a little hair at first,—

   A hair from her lover's head !

" It came in a gift of mignonette,

   And many a dainty bloom

Of briar and pink and violet,

   Whose perfume filled her room.

" She nourished it under the nightly dew,

   She fed it from her soul ;

And it grew and grew, until she knew

   That a viper was in the bowl !

" She nourished it through the evening hours ;

　She watched it day by day ;

She nourished it till the withered flowers

　Were culled and thrown away.

" She cherished it with a tender smile ;

　She touched it without fear ;

And I marvelled much that a thing so vile

　Should be to her so dear.

" ' Oh Hester, Hester ! my daughter sweet !

　The viper will work you harm ! '

But she trod my warning beneath her feet,

　And courted the awful charm.

" ' Oh father, father ! I may not scorn

　A creature that love hath made ;

For never was life so sweetly born,

　And I cannot be afraid.

" ' Oh, look at its glittering eyes ! " she said ;
　　They shine on me like stars !
And look at its dapples, so green and red,
　　And the sidelong, golden bars !

" ' Was ever a creature brave as this
　　By mortal maiden found ? '
The serpent raised his head with a hiss,
　　And merrily swam around !

" She laughed so loud, so long she laughed,
　　That I could nought but groan ;
For I knew my child was going daft
　　With the charm about her thrown.

" The bowl was strait for the noisome thing,
　　And it lengthened more and more,
Till it leaped, and lay in a mottled ring
　　Upon her chamber floor !

" All wonderful hues the rainbow knows
　Gleamed forth from its scaly skin,
And up from the centre its crest arose,
　And the tongue shot out and in !

" The moon was shining : I could not sleep :
　I clomb the silent stairs :
I sought her door in the midnight deep,
　And I caught her unawares !

" Fair as a lily she lay at rest
　In a flood of the ghostly sheen ;
Fair as twin lilies her virgin breast,
　And the serpent lay between ! "

Each maid rose shivering like a reed ;
　They stopped their ears with dread :
" Oh sir, thou hast lost thy wits, indeed !—
　Thou hast lost thy wits ! " they said.

(And one was Patience, so tall and fair;
  And one was queenly Prue;
And one was Hope with the golden hair;
  And the eyes of all were blue.)

He smote them down with a look of woe!
  " I shouted and shrieked amain!
It startled back like a bended bow,
  And slid from the counterpane!

" ' Oh Hester, Hester! how dare you lie
  With the thing upon your breast!'
And I waited to hear what mad reply
  Should break from the serpent's nest!

" ' Oh father dear! why come you here?'—
  She did not start or scream;
' The moon shines bright this time o' the year;
  I was dreaming a pleasant dream.'

" I answered her not; I turned around;
   I staggered to my bed;
And there I sank in a fearful swound,
   And lay as I were dead.

" But daily ever the monster grew,
   And lengthened hour by hour,
And lazily gloated as if it knew
   It held her in its power!

" It quivered in every golden flake,
   And grew in such degree,
That it seemed the snake which the moonbeams make,
   Crawling across the sea.

" A silken fillet, a cord, a rope,
   A Monster, a Thing of Doom,
It sucked the air of its life and hope,
   And crowded the tainted room.

" The midnight hour came round again ;
   The clock ticked like a bell ;
And I heard through all my burning brain
   The sound of a deed of hell !

" It wreathed its coils around her frame ;
   It lifted her in the air ;
And I heard the dragon as it came
   Slow creeping down the stair !

" It touched the latch, the door swung back ;
   It leaped the creaking sill ;
My head was split by a thunder-crack,
   And then the world was still !

" I could not move, I could not cry,
   But I knew my child was gone ;
Like a stone in the ground I seemed to lie,
   While the clock ticked on and on !

Out into the night they fled away—

  Out from the gaping door—

And the morning came with another day,

  But she came nevermore!

" But I saw it once! It reared its crest

  Where the sunset clouds were piled;

And I swear to Christ I will travel west

  Till I kiss once more my child!"

III.

The owl dropped out of his fainting hold,

  His head fell back aghast;

" Ah God!" shrieked the maidens, " thy tale is told,

  And we fear thy soul hath passed."

Guye lifted him in his arms amain;

  He bore him to his bed;

And the dear Lord eased him of his pain;

  In the midnight he was dead!

The storm grew weary along its path,
  The room was still and warm ;
But a storm arose of fiercer wrath
  Within each maiden's form.

It burst in bitterest tears and sighs;
  It shook them with its grief ;
They could not look in their father's eyes ;
  They could not find relief.

They left the dead in the flickering gloom
  They sought their chamber door ;
And they fearfully scanned the wintry room
  For the form their fancies bore.

They looked full long but did not find
  That monstrous form of Sin ;
(Yet a viper may lodge in a maiden's mind)
  And then they looked within.

The Puritan's Guest.

All doubtful shapes in hiding there
　　They killed in God's pure sight,
And they swept their penitent souls with prayer
　　That wild December night.

And when they woke on the morrow morn,
　　They worshipped—kneeling low—
And their souls were sweet as the day new-born,
　　And white as the drifted snow!

And one was Patience, so tall and fair;
　　And one was queenly Prue;
And one was Hope with the golden hair;
　　And the eyes of all were blue.

JACOB HURD'S CHILD.

I.

WHO breaketh his fast so early,
  While yet he can count the stars?
And whose are the footsteps trailing through
  The dew to the pasture-bars?

He snaffleth his white-eyed gelding,
  He mounteth the saddle-tree ;
And out from the skirts of Ipswich town
  All grimly rideth he.

Out from the town at sunrise,
  His stubborn fields untilled,
Rideth Jacob Hurd for a day and a night
  To see three witches killed.

For Hurd is a stalwart Christian
   Whom Satan hath ne'er enticed ;
He believeth in God and His holy word,
   And he hateth Antichrist.

The devil in awe he holdeth,
   And God with an equal fear ;
And little of Gospel and much of Law
   Make up his creed severe.

With a burning zeal for his Master,
   He fighteth with Death and Hell ;
And when a witch is brought to the rope,
   It pleaseth old Jacob well.

So out of the town at sunrise,
   His stubborn fields untilled,
He rideth forth for a day and a night
   To see three witches killed.

He glanceth backward at Ipswich,
  Then leaneth low to pray,
For he knoweth that in the wilderness
  The savage haunts the way.

Look for thy last, old Jacob !
  And pray, though thy prayer be vain ;
Thy errand hath not the smile of God ;
  Thou comest not again !

II.

It is four o'clock of the evening,
  And, dressed in her hodden gray,
Old Jacob's wife is humming a tune,
  For the goodman is away.

And forth from their distant cabins
  (None see them so soon as she),
The women who hold old Hurd in fear
  Are coming to drink her tea.

There's the pretty wife of Dunster,

   With Goffe's, from the meadow farm,

And the Sparhawke girls, with goodwife Gill,

   And the Glovers, arm in arm.

There is Peter Flynt's young widow,

   And her sister, in Lon'on brown,

And Miriam Winship : oh, sweet and wise

   Is the school-ma'am of the town !

And the heart of the goodwife, waiting

   The coming of friendly feet,

Is smitten through by an olden pang

   That is bitter at once, and sweet.

For the school-ma'am once taught him letters—

   The wonderful boy who died,

And who took from her motherly bosom all

   Its solace and its pride ;—

2

And Miriam's coming would surely
   Bring to her heart the joy
Of speaking, with none to make afraid,
   About her perished boy.

(For Jacob held hard to silence,
   Though he was more than sad,
And would not speak of their cruel loss
   With the mother of the lad.)

She meeteth them at her door-way
   With a greeting of hand to hand,
But she kisseth Miriam on her cheek,
   And the women understand.

III.

It is six o'clock of the evening,
   And, grouped at the table rude,
The women have bent their heads to say
   Their word of gratitude.

Now the tea and the feast are passing,
　While they gossip of home affairs—
Of the deacon's cattle in the pound,
　Or a sick child up for prayers;—

Of a work of grace in the village,
　⸰ And the devil's work abroad,
And the mischievous witches soon to go
　To the judgment-bar of God.

But Miriam speaketh a sentence
　That winneth the ears of all,
When she turneth her eyes on goodwife Hurd,
　And biddeth her talk of Paul.

Tears fill the eyes of the mother,
　And the kindly women list:
"The lips," said she, "should be good and wise
　That an angel's lips have kissed;

"But in truth my lips are neither;
  For God, by the hand of pain,
Sent a gift that my soul misunderstood,
  And he took it back again.

"For Jacob and I had prayed him
  That who should be born of me
Should·be sanctified at his birth, and strong
  In the power of prophecy.

"And the prayer was sweetly answered,
  But the prophet, all unguessed,
Grew weary of our clumsy ways,
  And entered into rest.

"It was better that he left us,
  For Jacob could not know,
That a child's sweet story was not a lie
  To be punished by a blow.

" For he was not made like others,

    His thoughts were weird and wild ;

  And Jacob at last believed, in truth,

    That a devil possessed the child.

" With the birds that gathered about him,

    He prattled for hours and hours ;

  He sang to the spider upon his web,

    And the bees in the hearts of flowers.

" He carried a curious wisdom ;

    And many were the times

  When he sat in the sun the livelong day,

    And sang to himself in rhymes.

" And he told such marvellous stories

    Of what he heard in the air,—

  Of the talk of the birds, and the songs of the sea,—

    That we were in despair.

" And Jacob exclaimed : ' God help us!

    For how is a man to know

  Whether a poet comes down from heaven,

    Or climbs from the world below?'

" One day, in the early autumn,

    When pigeons were in the woods,

  And out in the stubble the stripéd quail

    Were leading their pretty broods;

" When the partridge drummed in the distance,

    And the squirrel barked from the oak,

  And forth from the smoky hill-side came

    The woodman's lazy stroke,

" He went away toward tne forest,

    And I saw his face no more

  Till, flushed by the red of the setting sun,

    He stood in the cabin door.

Jacob Hurd's Child.

" ' Now where hast thou been ? ' said Jacob.
   ' I have been on my horse,' said he ;
And Jacob grew pale, and shook like a leaf
   As he took the lad on his knee.

" ' What horse hast thou ridden ? ' said Jacob.
   ' I have ridden my own,' he said—
' My golden horse with a silver tail,
   And a mane of silver thread.

" ' He came to me in the pasture,
   And he knelt for me to mount ;
And his saddle and bridle were blazing with
   More jewels than I could count.

" ' And he bore me like the lightning,
   Over sea and over land,
And he coursed the shore, or mounted the air,
   Or stopped at. my command.

" ' I have seen the windy ocean,
    And flown above its waves,
  And I've seen the great leviathan
    Playing within its caves.

" ' I have ridden through old England,
    Over hills and over dells,
  I have cantered through the London streets,
    And heard the London bells.

                        .

" ' I have been to the holy places,
    And knelt and prayed in them,
  And fed my golden horse with bread
    In the streets of Jerusalem.

" ' I have ridden by mighty rivers,
    From the mountains to the sea ;
  And hark ! ' said he, ' for my golden horse
    Is whinnying low for me ! '

" ' Get down !' said Jacob, fiercely ;

  " ' Thou knowest thou hast lied ;

    Surely the devil possesseth thee !'

And he smote him from his side.

" The sweet romancer staggered

    Into my waiting arms,

And I kissed his cheeks without a fear

    Of Satan or his charms.

" That night he lay in a fever,

    And raved of his golden horse ;

And Jacob sat and watched by him,

    In a helpless, dumb remorse.

" But my soul was in rebellion,

    For how could a child of prayer,

With the love of his mother in his heart,

    Be taken in such a snare ?

2*

" ' Thou believest that Mother Sewall
    Rideth a broom,' said I ;
' But thy darling talks of his golden horse,
    And thou smitest him for a lie.

" ' And I think, of the two, thou sinnest
    Against thy God the most ;
For I judge thou chargest the Evil One
    With the work of the Holy Ghost ! '

" But I begged my husband's pardon,
    For he was sore distraught ;
And would never leave the darling's bed,
    Though often I besought.

" Long days and nights thereafter,
    In his dream the sweet lad lay,
But his fancy was on its journeying,
    And always far away.

" And he spoke of wondrous countries
　Through which his journey led,
On his golden horse with the silver tail,
　And the mane of silver thread.

" Till Jacob and I believed him,
　And would not have marvelled much
Had the golden creature revealed himself
　To our credulous sight and touch.

" But weaker he grew and weaker,
　Until there came in his eye
A look so weary and worn, we knew
　Our little boy would die.

" One still and cloudy midnight
　He woke and gazed around,
And said that he heard his golden horse
　Pawing the pasture-ground.

" I think 'twas a bolt of thunder
    Shot by a distant shower,
  That shook the earth and the window-sash
    In the last throe of its power.

" And I think it was the lightning,
    That cheated our straining eyes ;
  But it seemed as if a beauteous horse
    Entered in golden guise,

" Breathing a flame from his nostrils,
    And pausing by the bed ;
  When the child sprang up with a cry of joy,
    And sank on his pillow, dead.

" And then, on the second morning,
    We bore him to the grave,—
  The child that we were unfit to keep,
    And had no power to save.

" But in the long procession,

    No eyes but ours could see

The wondrous figure we beheld

    Leading the company.

" For following hard the neighbors

    Who bore the precious corse,

Rode little Paul right gallantly

    Upon his golden horse.

" I saw him just as plainly

    As e'er I saw a flame ;

And he nodded to me with a smile,

    And Jacob saw the same."

IV.

The story and feast are ended,

    And forth from the open door,

With eyelids wide and faces flushed,

    The guests of the evening pour.

The sun in the west is setting,
  And bathing each farm and fold
With the lifted dust of the village ways
  In an atmosphere of gold.

Now what is that in the distance
  Which catches each gazing eye?
'Tis a flurry of dust that travels fast,
  Like a whirlwind from the sky!

Nearer it comes, and nearer,
  Till all the gazers know
That a horse is running without a man
  Behind the saddle-bow!

He courses along the highway
  That leads across the plain,
And they hear the beat of his heavy feet
  As he rushes down the lane.

And, leaning on Miriam Winship,
  A cry in her frightened breath,
The goodwife Hurd knows well that the horse
  Is the messenger of death ;

And that somewhere among the shadows
  Her husband lies apart,
With the scalp-lock riven from his head
  And an arrow in his heart.

And the women scream in wonder,
  For all can plainly see
That a little lad with a smiling face
  Bestrides the saddle-tree.

He tosses a kiss to his mother,
  He tenderly bows to all,
And they know that their eyes behold indeed,
  The spirit of little Paul.

The horse flies by the cottage,
  And into his pasture home,
Yellow and bright in the sunset gold,
  And spotted with silver foam.

And the women hasten homeward,
  Among the dropping dews,
To tell of the marvels they have seen,
  And to bear the heavy news.

But Miriam passeth inward,
  Her hand in goodwife Hurd's,
And readeth there, for her comforting,
  The Bible's gracious words.

Then reverently she kneeleth
  And uttereth a prayer,
That the childless and the widowed one
  May have the Father's care.

But ere her prayer she endeth,

  With fervent voice she saith:

" Oh punish not our blundering more

  With chastisement of death!

" But when thou sendest poets

  To such dull folk as we,

Inspire our blind and doubting eyes .

  To know them when we see!"

THE HEART OF THE WAR.

(1864.)

PEACE in the clover-scented air,
  And stars within the dome;
And underneath, in dim repose,
  A plain, New England home.
Within, a murmur of low tones
  And sighs from hearts oppressed,
Merging in prayer, at last, that brings
  The balm of silent rest.

———

I've closea a hard day's work, Marty,—
  The evening chores are done;
And you are weary with the house,
  And with the little one.

But he is sleeping sweetly now,

With all our pretty brood;

So come and sit upon my knee,

And it will do me good.

Oh, Marty! I must tell you all

The trouble in my heart,

And you must do the best you can

To take and bear your part.

You've seen the shadow on my face;

You've felt it day and night;

For it has filled our little home,

And banished all its light.

I did not mean it should be so,

And yet I might have known

That hearts which live as close as ours

Can never keep their own.

But we are fallen on evil times,
  And, do whate'er I may,
My heart grows sad about the war,
  And sadder every day.

I think about it when I work,
  And when I try to rest,
And never more than when your head
  Is pillowed on my breast;
For then I see the camp-fires blaze,
  And sleeping men around,
Who turn their faces toward their homes,
  And dream upon the ground.

I think about the dear, brave boys,
  My mates in other years,
Who pine for home and those they love,
  Till I am choked with tears.

With shouts and cheers they marched away
   On glory's shining track,
But, Ah! how long, how long they stay!
   How few of them come back!

One sleeps beside the Tennessee,
   And one beside the James,
And one fought on a gallant ship
   And perished in its flames.
And some, struck down by fell disease,
   Are breathing out their life ;
And others, maimed by cruel wounds,
   Have left the deadly strife.

Ah, Marty! Marty, only think
   Of all the boys have done
And suffered in this weary war !
   Brave heroes, every one !

Oh! often, often in the night,

I hear their voices call:

" *Come on and help us!   Is it right*

That we should bear it all? "

And when I kneel and try to pray,

My thoughts are never free,

But cling to those who toil and fight

And die for you and me.

And when I pray for victory,

It seems almost a sin

To fold my hands and ask for what

I will not help to win.

Oh! do not cling to me and cry,

For it will break my heart;

I'm sure you'd rather have me die

Than not to bear my part.

You think that some should stay at home
　To care for those away;
But still I'm helpless to decide
　If I should go or stay.

For, Marty, all the soldiers love,
　And all are loved again;
And I am loved, and love, perhaps,
　No more than other men.
I cannot tell—I do not know—
　Which way my duty lies,
Or where the Lord would have me build
　My fire of sacrifice.

I feel—I know—I am not mean;
　And, though I seem to boast,
I'm sure that I would give my life
　To those who need it most.

Perhaps the Spirit will reveal

That which is fair and right;

So, Marty, let us humbly kneel

And pray to Heaven for light.

———

Peace in the clover-scented air,

And stars within the dome;

And underneath, in dim repose,

A plain, New England home.

Within, a widow in her weeds,

From whom all joy is flown,

Who kneels among her sleeping babes,

And weeps and prays alone!

THE MARBLE PROPHECY.

THE harlequins are out in force to-day—
The piebald Swiss—and in the vestibule
Of great St. Peter's rings the rhythmic tread
Of Roman nobles, uniformed and armed
As the Pope's Guard ; and while their double line
With faultless curve enters the open door,
And sways and sparkles up the splendid nave,
Between the walls of humbler soldiery,
And parts to pass the altar—keeping step
To the proud beating of their Roman hearts—
A breeze of whispered admiration sweeps
The crowds that gaze, and dies within the dome

St. Peter's toe (the stump of it) was cold
An hour ago, but waxes warm apace

With rub of handkerchiefs, and dainty touch
Of lips and foreheads.

                    Smug behind their screen
Sits the Pope's Choir.   No woman enters there ;
For woman is impure, and makes impure
By voice and presence !   Mary, Mother of God !
Not thy own sex may sing thee in the courts
Of The All-Holy !—Only man, pure man !
Doubt not the purity of some of these—
Angels before their time—nor doubt
That they will sing like angels, when Papa,
Borne on the shoulders of his stalwart men
(The Master rode an ass), and canopied
By golden tapestries—the triple crown
Upon his brow, the nodding peacock plumes
Far heralding his way—shall come to take
His incense and his homage.

                         I will go.
'Tis a brave pageant, to be seen just once.

'Tis a brave pageant, but one does not like

To smutch his trousers kneeling to a man,

Or bide' the stare that follows if he fail :

So, having seen it once, one needs not wait.

What is the feast?   Let's see : ah ! I recall :

St. Peter's chair was brought from Antioch

So many years ago ;—the worse for wear

No doubt, and never quite luxurious,

But valued as a piece of furniture

By Rome above all price ; and so they give

High honor to the anniversary.

'Tis well ; in Rome they make account of. chairs.

If less in heaven, it possibly may be

Because they're greatly occupied by joy

Over bad men made penitent and pure

By this same chair ! Who knows?

I'll to the door !

The sun seems kind and simple in the sky

After such pomp. I thank thee, Sun! Thou hast

A smile like God, that reaches to the heart

Direct and sweet, without the ministries

Of scene and ceremonial! Thy rays

Fall not in benediction at the ends

Of two pale fingers; but thy warmth and light

Wrap well the cold dark world. I need no prism

To teach my soul that thou art beautiful:

It would divide thee, and confuse my sight.

Shine freely, sun! No mighty mother church

Stands mediator between thee and me!

Ay, shine on these—all these in shivering need—

To whom God's precious love is doled or sold

By sacerdotal hucksters! Shine on these,

And teach them that the God of Life and Light

Dwells not alone in temples made by hands;

And that the path to Him, from every soul,

In every farthest corner of the earth,

Is as direct as are thy rays to thee!

Ha! Pardon! Have I hurt you? Well-a-day!

I was not looking for a beggar here :—

Indeed, was looking upward ! But I see

You're here by royal license—with a badge

Made of good brass.   Come nearer to me ! there :

Take double alms, and give me chance to read

The number on your breast.   So : " Seventy-seven !"

'Tis a good number, man, and quite at home

About the temple.   Well, you have hard fare,

But many brothers and no end of shows !

Think it not ill that they will spend to-day,

Touching this chair, enough of time and gold

To gorge the poor of Rome.   The men who hold

The church in charge—who are, indeed, the church—

Have little time to give to starving men.

Be thankful for your label !   Only one

Can be the beggar " Number seventy-seven !"

They are distinguished persons : so are you !

You must be patient, though it seems, I grant,

A trifle odd that when a miracle

Is wrought before you, it will never take

A useful turn, as in the olden time,
And give you loaves and fishes, or increase
Your little dinners!

         Still the expectant crowds
Press up the street from round St. Angelo,
And thread the circling colonnade, or cross
With hurried steps the broad piazza—crowds
That pass the portal, and at once are lost
Within the vaulted glooms, as morning mist
Is quenched by morning air.

         It is God's house—
The noblest temple ever reared to Him
By hands of men—the culminating deed
Of a great church—the topmost reach of art
For the enshrinement of the Christian faith
In sign and symbol. Holiness becomes
The temple of the Holy!

         And these crowds?
Come they to pour the worship of their hearts

Like wine upon the altar? Who are they?

Last night, we hear, the theatre was full.

It was a spectacle : they went to see.

All yesterday they thronged the galleries,

Or roved among the ruins, or drove out

Upon the broad campagna—just to see.

This afternoon, with gaudy equipage,

(Their Bædeker and Murray left at home),

They'll be upon the Pincio—to see.

And so this morning, learning of the chair

And the Pope's coming, they are here to see

(The men in swallow-tails, their wives in black),

The grandest spectacle of all the week.

Make way ye men of poverty and dirt

Who fringe the outer lines ! Make open-way

And let them pass ! This is the House of God,

And swallow-tails are of fine moment here !

The ceremony has begun within.

I hear the far, faint voices of the choir,

As if a door in heaven were left ajar,

And cherubim were singing . . . Now I hear

The sharp, metallic chink of grounded arms

Upon the marble, as His Holiness

Moves up the lines of bristling bayonets

That guard his progress . . . But I stay alone.

Nay, I will to the Vatican, and there,

In converse with the thoughts of manlier men,

Pass the great morning! I shall be alone—

Ay, all alone with thee, Laocöon!

"A feast day and no entrance?" Can one's
  gold

Unloose a soul from purgatorial bonds

And ope the gates of heaven, without the power

To draw a bolt at the Museum? Wait!

Laocöon! thou great embodiment

Of human life and human history!

Thou record of the past, thou prophecy

Of the sad future, thou majestic voice,

Pealing along the ages from old time !

Thou wail of agonized humanity !

There lives no thought in marble like to thee !

Thou hast no kindred in the Vatican,

But standest separate among the dreams

Of old mythologics—alone—alone !

The beautiful Apollo at thy side

Is but a marble dream, and dreams are all

The gods and goddesses and fauns and fates

That populate these wondrous halls ; but thou,

Standing among them, liftest up thyself

In majesty of meaning, till they sink

Far from the sight, no more significant

Than the poor toys of children. For thou art

A voice from out the world's experience,

Speaking of all the generations past

To all the generations yet to come

Of the long struggle, the sublime despair,

The wild and weary agony of man !

3*

Ay, Adam and his offspring, in the toils

Of the twin serpents Sin and Suffering,

Thou dost impersonate ; and as I gaze

Upon the twining monsters that enfold

In unrelaxing, unrelenting coils,

Thy awful energies, and plant their fangs

Deep in thy quivering flesh, while still thy might

In fierce convulsion foils the fateful wrench

That would destroy thee, I am overwhelmed

With a strange sympathy of kindred pain,

And see through gathering tears the tragedy,

The curse and conflict of a ruined race !

Those Rhodian sculptors were gigantic men,

Whose inspirations came from other source

Than their religion, though they chose to speak

Through its familiar language,—men who saw,

And, seeing quite divinely, felt how weak

To cure the world's great woe were all the powers

Whose reign their age acknowledged. So they sat—

The immortal three—and pondered long and well

What one great work should speak the truth for them,—

What one great work should rise and testify

That they had found the topmost fact of life,

Above the reach of all philosophies

And all religions—every scheme of man

To placate or dethrone.   That fact they found,

And moulded into form.   The silly priest

Whose desecrations of the altar stirred

The vengeance of his God, and summoned forth

The wreathed gorgons of the slimy deep

To crush him and his children, was the word

By which they spoke to their own age and race,

That listened and applauded, knowing not

That high above the small significance

They apprehended, rose the grand intent

That mourned their doom and breathed a world's

    despair !

Be sure it was no fable that inspired

So grand an utterance.   Perchance some leal

From an old Hebrew record had conveyed

A knowledge of the genesis of man.

Perchance some fine conception rose in them

Of unity of nature and of race,

Springing from one beginning. Nay, perchance

Some vision flashed before their thoughtful eyes

Inspired by God, which showed the mighty man,

Who, unbegotten, had begot a race

That to his lot was linked through countless time

By living chains, from which in vain it strove

To wrest its tortured limbs and leap amain

To freedom and to rest! It matters not :

The double word—the fable and the fact,

The childish figment and the mighty truth,

Are blent in one. The first was for a day

And dying Rome ; the last for later time

And all mankind.

            These sculptors spoke their word

And then they died ; and Rome—imperial Rome—

The mistress of the world—debauched by blood

And foul with harlotries—fell prone at length

Among the trophies of her crimes and slept.

Down toppling one by one her helpless gods

Fell to the earth, and hid their shattered forms

Within the dust that bore them, and among

The ruined shrines and crumbling masonry

Of their old temples. Still this wondrous group,

From its long home upon the Esquiline,

Beheld the centuries of change, and stood,

Impersonating in its conscious stone

The unavailing struggle to crowd back

The closing folds of doom. It paused to hear

A strange New Name proclaimed among the
  streets,

And catch the dying shrieks of martyred men,

And see the light of hope and heroism

Kindling in many eyes ; and then it fell ;

And in the ashes of an empire swathed

Its aching sense, and hid its tortured forms.

The old life went, the new life came ; and Rome

That slew the prophets built their sepulchres,

And filled her heathen temples with the shrinés

Of Christian saints whom she had tossed to beasts,

Or crucified, or left to die in chains

Within her dungeons.   Ay, the old life went

But came again.   The primitive, true age—

The simple, earnest age—when Jesus Christ

The Crucified was only known and preached,

Struck hands with paganism and passed away.

Rome built new temples and installed new names ;

Set up her graven images, and gave

To Pope and priests the keeping of her gods.

Again she grasped at power no longer hers

By right of Roman prowess, and stretched out

Her hand upon the consciences of men.

The godlike liberty with which the Christ

Had made his people free she stole from them,

And bound them slaves to new observances.

Her times, her days, her ceremonials

Imposed a burden grievous to be borne,

And millions groaned beneath it. Nay, she grew

The vengeful persecutor of the free

Who would not bear her yoke, and bathed her hands

In blood as sweet as ever burst from hearts

Torn from the bosoms of the early saints

Within her Coliseum. She assumed

To be the arbiter of destiny.

Those whom she bound or loosed upon the earth,

Were bound or loosed in heaven! In God's own

      place,

She sat as God—supreme, infallible!

She shut the door of knowledge to mankind,

And bound the Word Divine. She sucked the juice

Of all prosperities within her realms,

Until her gaudy temples blazed with gold,

And from a thousand altars flashed the fire

Of priceless gems. To win her countless wealth

She sold as merchandise the gift of God.

She took the burden which the cross had borne,

And bound it fast to scourged and writhing loins

In thriftless Penance, till her devotees

Fled from their kind to find the boon of peace,

And died in banishment. Beneath her sway,

The proud old Roman blood grew thin and mean

Till virtue was the name it gave to fear,

Till heroism and brigandage were one,

And neither slaves nor beggars knew their shame !

What marvel that a shadow fell, world-wide,

And brooded o'er the ages? Was it strange

That in those dim and drowsy centuries,

When the dumb earth had ceased to quake beneath

The sounding wheels of progress, and the life

That erst had flamed so high had sunk so low

In cold monastic glooms and forms as cold,

The buried gods should listen in their sleep

And dream of resurrection? Was it strange

That listening well they should at length awake,

And struggle from their pillows? Was it strange

That men whose vision grovelled should perceive

The dust in motion, and with rapture greet

Each ancient deity with loud acclaim,

As if he brought with him the good old days

Of manly art and poetry and power?

Nay, was it strange that as they raised themselves,

And cleansed their drowsy eyelids of the dust,

And took their godlike attitudes again,

The grand old forms should feel themselves at
        home—

Saving perhaps a painful sense that men

Had dwindled somewhat? Was it strange, at last,

That all these gods should be installed anew,

And share the palace with His Holiness,

And that the Pope and Christian Rome can show

No art that equals that which had its birth

In pagan inspiration? Ah, what shame!

That after two millenniums of Christ,

Rome calls to her the thirsty tribes of earth,

And smites the heathen marble with her rod,

And bids them drink the best she has to give!

And when the gods were on their feet again

It was thy time to rise, Laocöon!

Those Rhodian sculptors had foreseen it all.

Their word was true : thou hadst the right to live.

In the quick sunlight on the Esquiline,

Where thou didst sleep, De Fredis kept his vines;

And long above thee grew the grapes whose blood

Ran wild in Christian arteries, and fed

The fire of Christian revels. Ah what fruit

Sucked up the marrow of thy marble there!

What fierce, mad dreams were those that scared the
     souls

Of men who drank, nor guessed what ichor stung

Their crimson lips, and tingled in their veins!

Strange growths were those that sprang above thy
     sleep :

Vines that were serpents ; huge and ugly trunks

That took the forms of human agony—

Contorted, gnarled and grim—and leaves that bore

The semblance of a thousand tortured hands,

And snaky tendrils that entwined themselves

Around all forms of life within their reach,

And crushed or blighted them !

                          At last the spade

Slid down to find the secret of the vines,

And touched thee with a thrill that startled Rome,

And swiftly called a shouting multitude

To witness thy unveiling.

                            Ah what joy

Greeted the rising from thy long repose !

And one, the mighty master of his time,

The king of Christian art, with strong, sad face

Looked on, and wondered with the giddy crowd,—

Looked on and learned (too late, alas ! for him),

That his humanity and God's own truth

Were more than Christian Rome, and spoke in words

Of larger import. Humbled Angelo

Bowed to the masters of the early days,

Grasped their strong hands across the centuries,

And went his way despairing !

                                Thou, meantime,

Didst find thyself installed among the gods

Here in the Vatican ; and thou, to-day,

Hast the same word for those who read thee well

As when thou wast created. Rome has failed :

Humanity is writhing in the toils

Of the old monsters as it writhed of old,

And there is neither help nor hope in her.

Her priests, her shrines, her rites, her mummeries,

Her pictures and her pageants, are as weak

To break the hold of Sin and Suffering

As those her reign displaced. Her iron hand

Shrivels the manhood it presumes to bless,

Drives to disgust or infidelity

The strong and free who dare to think and judge,

And wins a kiss from coward lips alone.

She does not preach the Gospel to the poor,

But takes it from their hands. The men who tread

The footsteps of the Master, and bow down

Alone to Him, she brands as heretics

Or hunts as fiends. She drives beyond her gates

The Christian worshippers of other climes,

And other folds and faiths, as if their brows

Were white with leprosy, and grants them there

With haughty scorn the privilege to kneel

In humble worship of the common Lord!

Is this the Christ, or look we still for Him?

Is the old problem solved, or lingers yet

The grand solution? Ay Laocöon!

Thy word is true, for Christian Rome has failed,

And I behold humanity in thee

As those who shaped thee saw it, when old Rome

In that far pagan evening fell asleep.

THE PALMER'S VISION.

Noon o'er Judea! All the air was beating
With the hot pulses of the day's great heart;
The birds were silent, and the rill retreating
Shrank in its covert, and complained apart,

When a lone pilgrim, with his scrip and burdon,
Dropped by the wayside, weary and distressed,
His sinking heart grown faithless of its guerdon—
The city of his recompense and rest.

No vision yet of Galilee and Tabor!
No glimpse of distant Zion throned and crowned!
Behind him stretched his long and useless labor,
Before him lay the parched and stony ground.

He leaned against à shrine of Mary, casting
Its balm of shadow on his aching head,
And worn with toil, and faint with cruel fasting,
He sighed: "O God! O God, that I were dead!

"The friends I loved are lost or left behind me;
In penury and loneliness I roam;
These endless paths of penance choke and blind me;
Oh come and take thy wasted pilgrim home!"

Then with the form of Mary bending o'er him,
Her hands in changeless benediction stayed,
The palmer slept, while a swift dream upbore him
To the fair paradise for which he prayed.

He stood alone, wrapped in divinest wonder;
He saw the pearly gates and jasper walls
Informed with light, and heard the far-off thunder
Of chariot wheels and mighty waterfalls!

From far and near, in rhythmic palpitations,
Rose on the air the noise of shouts and psalms;
And through the gates he saw the ransomed nations,
Marching and waving their triumphant palms.

And white within the thronging Empyrean,
A golden palm-branch in his kingly hand,
He saw his Lord, the gracious Galilean,
Amid the worship of his myriads stand!

"O Jesus! Lord of glory! Bid me enter!
I worship thee! I kiss thy holy rood!"
The pilgrim cried, when from the burning centre
'A broad-winged angel sought him where he stood.

"Why art thou here?" in accents deep and tender
Outspoke the messenger. "Dost thou not know
That none may win the city's rest and splendor,
Who do not cut their palms in Jericho?

" Go back to earth, thou palmer empty-handed !

Go back to hunger and the toilsome way !

Complete the task that duty hath commanded,

And win the palm thou hast not brought to-day ! "

And then the sleeper woke, and gazed around him ;

Then springing to his feet with life renewed,

He spurned the faithless weakness that had bound him,

And, faring on, his pilgrimage pursued.

The way was hard, and he grew halt and weary,

But one long day, among the evening hours,

He saw beyond a landscape gray and dreary

The sunset flame on Salem's sacred towers !

O, fainting soul that readest well this story,

Longing through pain for death's benignant balm,

Think not to win a heaven of rest and glory

If thou shalt reach its gates without thy palm !

4

TO WHITTIER ON HIS SEVENTIETH BIRTHDAY.

TEN gentle-hearted boys of seven,

Too young and sweet to stray from heaven,

Will—counting up the little men—

Amount to three score years and 'ten.

Two gracious men of thirty-five,

With wits alert and hearts alive,

Will fill complete the rounded spheres

Of seventy strong and manly years.

Nay, Whittier, thou art not old ;

Thy register a lie hath told,

For lives devote to love and truth

Do only multiply their youth.

Thou art ten gentle boys of seven,

With souls too sweet to stray from heaven;

Thou art two men of thirty-five,

With wits alert, and hearts alive!

A GLIMPSE OF YOUTH.

MAIDEN, I thank thee for thy face,
Thy sweet, shy glance of conscious eyes;
For, from thy beauty and thy grace,
My life has won a glad surprise.

I met thee on the crowded street—
A load of care on heart and brain—
And, for a moment, bright and fleet,
The vision made me young again.

And then I thought, as on I went,
And struggled through the thronging ways,
How every age's complement
The age that follows overlays.

The youth upon the child shuts down ;

Young manhood closes over youth ;

And ripe old age is but the crown

That keeps them both in changeless truth !

So, every little child I see,

With brow and spirit undefiled,

And simple faith and frolic glee,

Finds still in me another child.

Toward every brave and careless boy

Whose lusty shout or call I hear,

The boy within me springs with joy

And rings an echo to his cheer !

What was it, when thy face I saw,

That moved my spirit like a breeze,

Responsive to the primal law

Of youth's entrancing harmonies?

Ah! little maid—so sweet and shy—
Building each day thy fair romance—
Thou didst not dream a youth passed by,
When I returned thee glance for glance!

For all my youth is still my own,—
Bound in the volume of my age,—
And breath from thee hath only blown
The leaves back to the golden page!

A GOLDEN WEDDING-SONG.

THE links of fifty golden years
  Reach to the golden ring
Which now, with glad and grateful tears,
  We celebrate and sing,
O chain of love ! O ring of gold !
  That have the years defied ;
And still in happy bondage hold
  The old man and his bride !

The locks are white that once were black ;
  The sight is feebler grown ;
But through the long and weary track
  The heart has held its own !

O chain of love! O ring of gold!

That time could not divide;

That kept through changes manifold

The old man with his bride!

The little ones have come and gone;

The old have passed away;

But love—immortal love—lives on,

And blossoms 'mid decay.

O chain of love! O ring of gold!

That have the years defied;

And still with growing strength infold

The old man and his bride!

The golden bridal! ah, how sweet

The music of its bell,

To those whose hearts the vows repeat

Their lives have kept so well!

O chain of love ! O ring of gold !

O marriage true and tried !

That bind with tenderness untold

The old man to his bride !

4*

DANIEL GRAY.

IF I shall ever win the home in heaven
For whose sweet rest I humbly hope and pray,
In the great company of the forgiven
I shall be sure to find old Daniel Gray.

I knew him well; in truth, few knew him better;
For my young eyes oft read for him the Word,
And saw how meekly from the crystal letter
He drank the life of his beloved Lord.

Old Daniel Gray was not a man who lifted
On ready words his freight of gratitude,
Nor was he called among the gifted,
In the prayer-meetings of his neighborhood.

He had a few old-fashioned words and phrases,

Linked in with sacred texts and Sunday rhymes ;

And I suppose that in his prayers and graces,

I've heard them all at least a thousand times.

I see him now—his form, his face, his motions,

His homespun habit, and his silver hair,—

And hear the language of his trite devotions,

Rising behind the straight-backed kitchen chair.

I can remember how the sentence sounded—

"Help us, O Lord, to pray and not to faint!"

And how the "conquering-and-to-conquer" rounded

The loftier aspirations of the saint.

He had some notions that did not improve him,

He never kissed his children—so they say ;

And finest scenes and fairest flowers would move him

Less than a horse-shoe picked up in the way.

He had a hearty hatred of oppression,
And righteous words for sin of every kind;
Alas, that the transgressor and transgression
Were linked so closely in his honest mind!

He could see naught but vanity in beauty,
And naught but weakness in a fond caress,
And pitied men whose views of Christian duty
Allowed indulgence in such foolishness.

Yet there were love and tenderness within him;
And I am told that when his Charlie died,
Nor nature's need nor gentle words could win him
From his fond vigils at the sleeper's side.

And when they came to bury little Charlie,
They found fresh dew-drops sprinkled in his hair,
And on his breast a rose-bud gathered early,
And guessed, but did not know who placed it there.

Honest and faithful, constant in his calling,
Strictly attendant on the means of grace,
Instant in prayer, and fearful most of falling,
Old Daniel Gray was always in his place.

A practical old man, and yet a dreamer,
He thought that in some strange, unlooked-for way
His mighty Friend in Heaven, the great Redeemer,
Would honor him with wealth some golden day.

This dream he carried in a hopeful spirit
Until in death his patient eye grew dim,
And his Redeemer called him to inherit
The heaven of wealth long garnered up for him.

So, if I ever win the home in heaven
For whose sweet rest I humbly hope and pray,
In the great company of the forgiven
I shall be sure to find old Daniel Gray.

MERLE THE COUNSELLOR.

OLD MERLE, the counsellor and guide,
And tall young Rolfe walked side by side
At the sweet hour of eventide.

The yellow light of parting day
Upon the peaceful landscape lay,
And touched the mountain far away.

The tinkling of the distant herds,
And the low twitter of the birds
Mingled with childhood's happy words.

The old man raised his trembling palm,
And bared his brow to meet the balm
That fell with twilight's dewy calm;

And one could see that to his thought,

The scenes and sounds around him brought

Suggestions of the heaven he sought.

But Rolfe, his young companion, bent

His moody brow in discontent,

And sadly murmured as he went.

For vagrant passions, fierce and grim,

And fearful memories haunted him,

That made the evening glory dim.

Then spoke the cheerful voice of Merle :

"Where yonder clouds their gold unfurl,

One almost sees the gates of pearl.

"Nay, one can hardly look amiss

For heaven, in such a scene as this,

Or fail to feel its present bliss.

" So near we stand to holy things,
　　And all our high imaginings,
　　That faith forgets to lift her wings ! "

　　Then answered Rolfe, with bitter tone :
" If·thou hast visions of the throne,
　　Enjoy them ; they are all thy own.

" For me there lives no God of love ;
　　For me there bends no heaven above ;
　　And Peace, the gently brooding dove,

" Has flown afar, and in her stead
　　Fierce vultures wheel above my head,
　　And hope is sick and faith is dead.

" Death can but loose a loathsome bond,
　　And from the depths of my despond,
　　I see no ray of light beyond."

It was a sad, discordant strain,

That brought old Merle to earth again,

And filled his soul with solemn pain.

At length they reached a leafy wood,

And walked in silence, till they stood

Within the fragrant solitude.

Then spake old Merle with gentle art :

" I know the secret of thy heart,

And will, if thou desire, impart."

Rolfe answered with a hopeless sigh,

But from the tear that brimmed his eye,

The old man gladly caught reply,

And spoke : " Beyond these forest trees

A city stands ; and sparkling seas

Waft up to it the evening breeze,

" Thou canst not see its gilded domes,

    Its plume of smoke, its pleasant homes,

    Or catch the gleam of surf that foams

" And dies upon its verdant shore,

    But there it stands ; and there the roar

    Of life shall swell for evermore !

" The path we walk is fair and wide,

    But still our vision is denied

    The city and its nursing tide.

" The path we walk is wide and fair,

    But curves and wanders here and there,

    And builds the wall of our despair.

" Make straight the path, and then shall shine

    Through trembling walls of tree and vine

    The vision fair for which we pine.

"And thou, my son, so long hast been

    Along the crooked ways of sin,

    That they have closed, and shut thee in.

"Make straight the path before thy feet,

    And walk within it firm and fleet,

    And thou shalt see, in vision sweet

"And constant as the love supreme,

    With closer gaze and brighter beam,

    The peaceful heaven that fills my dream."

He paused : no more his lips could say ;

    And then, beneath the twilight gray,

    The silent pair retraced their way.

But in the young man's eyes a light

    Shone strong and resolute and bright,

    For which Merle thanked his God that night.

WANTED.

GOD give us men! A time like this demands
Strong minds, great hearts, true faith, and ready hands;
Men whom the lust of office does not kill;
  Men whom the spoils of office cannot buy;
Men who possess opinions and a will;
  Men who have honor,—men who will not lie;
Men who can stand before a demagogue,
  And damn his treacherous flatteries without winking!
Tall men, sun-crowned, who live above the fog
  In public duty, and in private thinking:
For while the rabble, with their thumb-worn creeds,
Their large professions and their little deeds,—
Mingle in selfish strife, lo! Freedom weeps,
Wrong rules the land, and waiting Justice sleeps!

VERSES READ AT THE HADLEY CENTENNIAL.

(JUNE 9, 1859.)

HEART of Hadley, slowly beating

Under midnight's azure breast,

Silence thy strong pulse repeating

Wakes me—shakes me—from my rest.*

Hark! a beggar at the basement!

Listen! friends are at the door!

There's a lover at the casement!

There are feet upon the floor!

---

* The pulsations of Hadley Falls, on the Connecticut, are felt for many miles around, in favorable conditions of the atmosphere.

But they knock with muffled hammers,

They step softly like the rain,

And repeat their gentle clamors

Till I sleep and dream again.

Still the knocking at the basement ;

Still the rapping at the door ;

Tireless lover at the casement ;

Ceaseless feet upon the floor.

Bolts are loosed by spectral fingers,

Windows open through the gloom,

And the lilacs and syringas

Breathe their perfume through the room.

'Mid the odorous pulsations

Of the air around my bed,

Throng the ghostly generations

Of the long forgotten dead.

"Rise and write!" with gentle pleading
    They command, and I obey;
And I give to you the reading
    Of their tender words to-day:

"Children of the old plantation,
    Heirs of all we won and held,
Greet us in your celebration—
    Us—the nameless ones of Eld!

"We were never squires or teachers,
    We were neither wise nor great,
But we listened to our preachers,
    Worshipped God and loved the State.

"Blood of ours is on the meadow,
    Dust of ours is in the soil,
But no marble casts a shadow
    Where we slumber from our toil.

" Unremembered, unrecorded,

   We are sleeping side by side,

And to names is now awarded

   That for which the nameless died.

" We were men of humble station ;

   We were women pure and true ;

And we served our generation,—

   Lived and worked and fought for you.

" We were maidens, we were lovers,

   We were husbands, we were wives ;

But oblivion's mantle covers

   All the sweetness of our lives.

" Praise the men who ruled and led us ;

   Carry garlands to their graves ;

But remember that your meadows

   Were not planted by their slaves.

" Children of the old plantation,

    Heirs of all we won and held,

Greet us in your celebration,—

    Us, the nameless ones of Eld."

This their message, and I send it,

    Faithful to their sweet behest,

And my toast shall e'en attend it,

    To be read among the rest.

Fill to all the brave and blameless

    Who, forgotten, passed away!

Drink the memory of the nameless,—

    Only named in heaven to-day!

5

A CHRISTMAS CAROL.

THERE'S a song in the air !

There's a star in the sky !

There's a mother's deep prayer

And a baby's low cry !

And the star rains its fire while the Beautiful sing,

For the manger of Bethlehem cradles a king.

There's a tumult of joy

O'er the wonderful birth,

For the virgin's sweet boy

Is the Lord of the earth,

Ay ! the star rains its fire and the Beautiful sing,

For the manger of Bethlehem cradles a king !

In the light of that star

Lie the ages impearled ;

And that song from afar

Has swept over the world.

Every hearth is aflame, and the Beautiful sing

In the homes of the nations that Jesus is King.

We rejoice in the light,

And we echo the song

That comes down through the night

From the heavenly throng.

Ay ! we shout to the lovely evangel they bring,

And we greet in his cradle our Saviour and King !

THE OLD CLOCK OF PRAGUE.

THERE'S a curious clock in the city of Prague—
A remarkable old astronomical clock—
With a dial whose outline is that of an egg,
And with figures and fingers a wonderful stock.

It announces the dawn and the death of the day,
Shows the phases of moons and the changes of tides,
Counts the months and the years as they vanish away,
And performs quite a number of marvels besides.

At the left of the dial a skeleton stands ;
And aloft hangs a musical bell in the tower,
Which he rings, by a rope that he holds in his hands,
In his punctual function of striking the hour.

And the skeleton nods, as he tugs at the rope,

    At an odd little figure that eyes him aghast,

As a hint that the bell rings the knell of his hope,

    And the hour that is solemnly tolled is his last.

And the effigy turns its queer features away

    (Much as if for a snickering fit or a sneeze),

With a shrug and a shudder, that struggle to say :

    " Pray excuse me, but—just an hour more, if you

        please ! "

But the funniest sight, of the numerous sights

    Which the clock has to show to the people below,

Is the Holy Apostles in tunics and tights,

    Who revolve in a ring, or proceed in a row.

Their appearance can hardly be counted sublime ;

    And their movements are formal, it must be allowed ;

But they're prompt, for they always appear upon time,

    And polite, for they bow very low to the crowd.

This machine (so reliable papers record)

   Was the work, from his own very clever design

Of one Hanusch, who died in the year of our Lord

   One thousand four hundred and ninety and nine.

Did the people receive it with honor? you ask;

   Did it bring a reward to the builder? Ah, well!

It was proper that they should have paid for the task!

   And they did, in a way that it shocks me to tell.

For suspecting that Hanusch might grow to be vain,

   Or that cities around them might covet their prize,

They invented a story that he was insane,

   And, to stop him from labor, extinguished his eyes!

But the cunning old artist, though dying in shame,

   May be sure that he labored and lived not amiss;

For his clock has outlasted the foes of his fame,

   And the world owes him much for a lesson like this:

That a private success is a public offence,

That a citizen's fame is a city's disgrace,

And that both should be shunned by a person of sense

Who would live with a whole pair of eyes in his face.

ALBERT DURER'S STUDIO.

In the house of Albert Durer
　Still is seen the studio
Where the pretty Nurembergers
　(Cheeks of rose and necks of snow)
Sat to have their portraits painted,
　Thrice a hundred years ago.

Still is seen the little loop-hole
　Where Frau Durer's jealous care
Watched the artist at his labor,
　And the sitter in her chair,
To observe each word and motion
　That should pass between the pair.

Handsome, hapless Albert Durer
　Was as circumspect and true
As the most correct of husbands,
　When the dear delightful shrew
Has him, and his sweet companions,
　Every moment under view.

But I trow that Albert Durer
　Had within his heart a spot
Where he sat, and painted pictures
　That gave beauty to his lot,
And the sharp, intrusive vision
　Of Frau Durer entered not.

Ah! if brains and hearts had loop-holes,
　And Frau Durer could have seen
All the pictures that his fancy
　Hung upon their walls within,
How minute had been her watching,
　And how good he would have been !
　5*

ALONE.

ALL alone in the world! all alone!
With a child on my knee, or a wife on my breast,
Or, sitting beside me, the beautiful guest
Whom my heart leaps to greet as its sweetest and
    best,
    Still alone in the world! all alone!

    With my visions of beauty, alone!
Too fair to be painted, too fleet to be scanned,
Too regal to stay at my feeble command,
They pass from the grasp of my impotent hand :
    Still alone in the world! all alone!

Alone with my conscience, alone!

Not an eye that can see when its finger of flame

Points my soul to its sin, or consumes it with shame!

Not an ear that can hear its low whisper of blame!

    Still alone in the world! all alone!

In my visions of self, all alone!

The weakness, the meanness, the guilt that I see,

The fool or the fiend I am tempted to be,

Can only be seen and repented by me :

    Still alone in the world! all alone!

Alone in my worship, alone!

No hand in the universe, joining with mine,

Can lift what it lays on the altar divine,

Or bear what it offers aloft to its shrine :

    Still alone in the world! all alone!

In the valley of death, all alone!

The sighs and the tears of my friends are in vain,

For mine is the passage, and mine is the pain,

And mine the sad sinking of bosom and brain :

    Still alone in the world! all alone!

Not alone! never, never alone!

There is one who is with me by day and by night,

Who sees and inspires all my visions of light,

And teaches my conscience its office aright:

    Not alone in the world! not alone!

Not alone! never, never alone!

He sees all my weakness with pitying eyes,

He helps me to lift my faint heart to the skies,

And in my last passion he suffers and dies:

    Not alone! never, never alone!

SONG AND SILENCE.

'My Mabel, you once had a bird

   In your throat; and it sang all the day!

   But now it sings never a word :

     Has the bird flown away ?

"Oh sing to me, Mabel, again!

   Strike the chords! Let the old fountain flow

   With its balm for my fever and pain,

     As it did years ago!"

Mabel sighed (while a tear filled and fell,)

"I have bade all my singing adieu;

   But I've a true story to tell,

     And I'll tell it to you.

"There's a bird's nest up there in the oak,
 On the bough that hangs over the stream,
And last night the mother-bird broke
 Into song in her dream.

"This morning she woke, and was still;
 For she thought of the frail little things
That needed her motherly bill,
 Waiting under her wings.

"And busily, all the day long,
 She hunted and carried their food,
And forgot both herself and her song
 In her care for her brood.

"I sang in my dream, and you heard:
 I woke, and you wonder I'm still;
But a mother is always a bird
 With a fly in its bill!"

WHERE SHALL THE BABY'S DIMPLE BE ?

OVER the cradle the mother hung,

Softly crooning a slumber-song;

And these were the simple words she sung

All the evening long:

" Cheek or chin, or knuckle or knee,

Where shall the baby's dimple be?

Where shall the angel's finger rest

When he comes down to the baby's nest?

Where shall the angel's touch remain

When he awakens my babe again?"

Still as she bent and sang so low,

A murmur into her music broke;

And she paused to hear, for she could but know

The baby's angel spoke.

"Cheek or chin, or knuckle or knee,

Where shall the baby's dimple be?

Where shall my finger fall and rest

When I come down to the baby's nest?

Where shall my finger's touch remain

When I awaken your babe again?"

Silent the mother sat, and dwelt

Long in the sweet delay of choice;

And then by her baby's side she knelt,

And sang with pleasant voice:

" Not on the limb, O angel dear!

For the charm with its youth will disappear;

Not on the cheek shall the dimple be,

For the harboring smile will fade and flee;

But touch thou the chin with an impress deep,

And my baby the angel's seal shall keep."

TO A SLEEPING SINGER.

LOVE in her heart, and song upon her lip—
A daughter, friend, and wife—
She lived a beauteous life,
And love and song shall bless her in her sleep.
The flowers whose language she interpreted,
The delicate airs, calm eves, and starry skies
That touched so sweetly her chaste sympathies,
And all the grieving souls she comforted,
Will bathe in separate sorrows the dear mound,
Where heart and harp lie silent and profound.
Oh, Woman! all the songs thou left to us
We will preserve for thee, in grateful love;
Give thou return of our affection thus,
And keep for us the songs thou sing'st above!

EUREKA.

WHOM I crown with love is royal;

Matters not her blood or birth;

She is queen, and I am loyal

To the noblest of the earth.

Neither place, nor wealth, nor title,

Lacks the man my friendship owns;

His distinction, true and vital,

Shines supreme o'er crowns and thrones.

Where true love bestows its sweetness,

Where true friendship lays its hand,

Dwells all greatness, all completeness,

All the wealth of every land.

Man is greater than condition,
  And where man himself bestows,
He begets, and gives position
  To the gentlest that he knows.

Neither miracle nor fable
  Is the water changed to wine;
Lords and ladies at my table
  Prove Love's simplest fare divine.

And if these accept my duty,
  If the loved my homage own,
I have won all worth and beauty;
  I have found the magic stone.

RETURNING CLOUDS.

THE clouds are returning after the rain.
  All the long morning they steadily sweep
From the blue Northwest, o'er the upper main,
  In a peaceful flight to their Eastern sleep.

With sails that the cool wind fills or furls,
  And shadows that darken the billowy grass,
Freighted with amber, or piled with pearls,
  Fleets of fair argosies rise and pass.

The earth smiles back to the smiling throng
  From greening pasture and blooming field,
For the earth that had sickened with thirst so long
  Has been touched by the hand of The Rain, and
    healed.

The old man sits neath the tall elm trees,
  And watches the pageant with dreamy eyes,
While his white locks stir to the same cool breeze
  That scatters the silver along the skies.

The old man's eyelids are wet with tears—
  Tears of sweet pleasure and sweeter pain—
For his thoughts are driving back over the years
  In beautiful clouds after life's long rain.

Sorrows that drowned all the springs of his life,
  Trials that crushed him with pitiless beat,
Storms of temptation and tempests of strife,
  Float o'er his memory tranquil and sweet.

And the old man's spirit, made soft and bright
  By the long, long rain that had bent him low,
Sees a vision of angels on wings of white,
  In the trooping clouds as they come and go.

GRADATIM.

HEAVEN is not reached at a single bound ;
   But we build the ladder by which we rise
   From the lowly earth to the vaulted skies,
And we mount to its summit round by round.

I count this thing to be grandly true :
   That a noble deed is a step toward God,—
   Lifting the soul from the common clod
To a purer air and a broader view.

We rise by the things that are under feet ;
   By what we have mastered of good and gain ;
   By the pride deposed and the passion slain,
And the vanquished ills that we hourly meet.

We hope, we aspire, we resolve, we trust,

When the morning calls us to life and light,

But our hearts grow weary, and, ere the night,

Our lives are trailing the sordid dust.

We hope, we resolve, we aspire, we pray,

And we think that we mount the air on wings

Beyond the recall of sensual things,

While our feet still cling to the heavy clay.

Wings for the angels, but feet for men!

We may borrow the wings to find the way—

We may hope, and resolve, and aspire, and pray;

But our feet must rise, or we fall again.

Only in dreams is a ladder thrown

From the weary earth to the sapphire walls;

But the dreams depart, and the vision falls,

And the sleeper wakes on his pillow of stone.

Heaven is not reached at a single bound;

But we build the ladder by which we rise

From the lowly earth to the vaulted skies,

And we mount to its summit, round by round.

ON THE RIGHI.

On the Righi Kulm we stood,
  Lovely Floribel and I,
While the morning's crimson flood
  Streamed along the eastern sky.
Reddened every mountain peak
  Into rose, from twilight dun;
But the blush upon her cheek
  Was not lighted by the sun!

On the Righi Kulm we sat,
  Lovely Floribel and I,
Plucking blue-bells for her hat
  From a mound that blossomed nigh.
6

" We are near to heaven," she sighed,

    While her raven lashes fell.

" Nearer," softly I replied,

    " Than the mountain's height may tell."

Down the Righi's side we sped.

    Lovely Floribel and I,

But her morning blush had fled,

    And the blue-bells all were dry.

Of the height the dream was born;

    Of the lower air it died;

And the passion of the morn

    Flagged and fell at eventide.

From the breast of blue Lucerne,

    Lovely Floribel and I

Saw the brand of sunset burn

    On the Righi Kulm, and die.

And we wondered, gazing thus,

   If our dream would still remain

On the height, and wait for us

   Till we climb to heaven again!

THE WINGS.

A FEEBLE wail was heard at night,
  And a stifled cry of joy ;
And when the morn broke cool and light,
They bore to the mother's tearful sight
  A fair and lovely boy.

Months passed away;
And day by day
  The mother hung about her child
As in his little cot he lay,
  And watched him as he smiled,
And threw his hands into the air,
  And turned above his large, bright eyes,
With an expression half of prayer
And half of strange surprise ;

For hovering o'er his downy head
A dainty vision hung.
Fluttering, swaying,
Unsteadily it swung,
As if suspended by a thread,
His own sweet breath obeying.

Sometimes with look of wild beseeching
He marked it as it dropped
Almost within his awkward reaching,
And as the vision stopped
Beyond his anxious grasp,
And cheated the quick clasp
Of dimpled hands, and quite
Smothered his chirrup of delight,

And he saw his effort vain
And the bright vision there again

Dancing before his sight,

   His eyes grew dim with **tears,**

   Till o'er the flooded spheres

     The soothing eyelids crept,

     And the tired infant slept.

He saw—his mother could not **see—**

A presence and a mystery :

     Two waving wings,

Spangled with silver, starlike things :

     No form of light was borne between ;

     Only the wings were seen !

Years steal away with silent feet,

   And he, the little one,

With brow more fair and voice more sweet

   Is playing in the sun.

Flowers are around him and the songs

   Of bounding streams and happy birds,

But sweeter than their sweetest tongues

Break forth his own glad words.

And as he sings

The wings, the wings!

Before him still they fly!

And nothing that the summer brings

Can so entice his eye.

Hovering here, hovering there,

Hovering everywhere,

They flash and shine among the flowers,

While dripping sheen in golden showers

Falls through the air where'er they hover

Upon the radiant things they cover.

Hurrying here, hurrying there,

Hurrying everywhere,

He plucks the flowers they shine upon,

But while he plucks their light is gone!

And casting down the faded things,

Onward he springs

To follow the wings!

Years run away with silent feet;
  The boy, to manhood grown,
Within a shadowy retreat
  Stands anxious and alone.
His bosom heaves with heavy sighs,
  His hair hangs damp and long,
But fiery purpose fills his eyes,
  And his limbs are large and strong:
  And there above a gentle hill,
  The wings are hovering still,
  While their soft radiance, rich and warm,
  Falls on a maiden's form.

  And see! again he starts,
  And onward darts,
Then pauses with a fierce and sudden pain,
  Then presses on again,
Till with mixed thoughts of rapture and despair,
  He kneels before her there:—

With hands together prest,
He prays to her with low and passionate calls,
And, like a snow-flake pure, she flutters, falls,
And melts upon his breast.

Long in that dearest trance he hung—
Then raised his eyes; the wings that swung
In glancing circles round his head
Afar had fled,
And wheeled, with calm and graceful flight,
Over a scene
That glowed with glories beauteously bright
Beneath their sheen.

High in the midst a monument arose,
Of pale enduring marble; calm and still,
It seemed a statue of sublime repose,
The silent speaker of a mighty will.
6*

Its sides were hung around
With boughs of evergreen; and its long shaft was
   crowned
   With a bright laurel-wreath,
   And glittering beneath
Were piled great heaps of gold upon the ground.

Children were playing near—fair boys and girls,
   Who shook their sunny curls,
And laughed and sang in mirthfulness of spirit,
   And in their childish pleasures
   Danced around the treasures
Of gold and honor they were to inherit.

   The sight has fired his brain;
   Onward he springs again.
   O'er ruined blocks
   Of wild and perilous rocks,
Through long damp caves, o'er pitfalls dire,
And maddening scenes of blood and fire,

Fainting with heat,

Benumbed with cold,

With weary, aching feet,

He sternly toils, and presses on to greet

The monument, the laurels and the gold.

Years have passed by; a shattered form

Leans faintly on a monument;

His glazing eyes are bent

In sadness down: a tear falls to the ground

That through the furrows of his cheek hath wound.

The children beautiful have ceased to play,

Tarnished the marble stands with dark decay,

The laurels all are dead, and flown the gold away.

Once more he raised his eyes; before him lay

A dim and lonely vale,

And feebly tottering in the downward way

Walked spectres cold and pale.

And darkling groves of shadowy cypress sprung

Among the damp clouds that around them hung.

One vision only cheers his aching sight;
 Those wings of light
Have lost their varied hues, and changed to white,
 And, with a gentle motion, slowly wave
  Over a new made grave.
He casts one faltering, farewell look behind,
Around, above, one mournful glance he throws,
Then with a cheerful smile, and trusting mind,
Moves feebly toward the valley of repose.
He stands above the grave; dull shudders creep
Along his limbs, cold drops are on his brow;
One sigh he heaves, and sinking into sleep
He drops and disappears;—and dropping now,
 The wings have followed too.
 But, lo! new visions burst upon the view!
 They reappear in glory bright and new!
 And to their sweet embrace a soul is given,
And on the wings of HOPE an angel flies to HEAVEN.

INTIMATIONS.

WHAT glory then! What darkness now!
  A glimpse, a thrill, and it is flown!
  I reach, I grasp, but stand alone,
With empty arms and upward brow!

Ye may not see, O weary eyes!
  The band of angels, swift and bright,
  That pass, but cannot wake your sight,
Down trooping from the crowded skies.

O heavy ears! Ye may not hear
  The strains that pass my conscious soul,
  And seek, but find no earthly goal,
Far falling from another sphere.

Ah! soul of mine! Ah! soul of mine!
   Thy sluggish senses are but bars
   That stand between thee and the stars,
And shut thee from the world divine.

For something sweeter far than sound,
   And something finer than the light
   Comes through the discord and the night
And penetrates, or wraps thee round.

Nay, God is here, couldst thou but see;
   All things of beauty are of Him;
   And heaven, that holds the cherubim,
As lovingly embraces thee!

If thou hast apprehended well
   The tender glory of a flower,
   Which moved thee, by some subtle power
Whose source and sway thou couldst not tell;

If thou hast kindled to the sweep

  Of stormy clouds across the sky,

  Or gazed with tranced and tearful eye,

And swelling breast, upon the deep ;

If thou hast felt the throb and thrill

  Of early day and happy birds,

  While peace, that drowned thy chosen words

Has flowed from thee in glad good-will,

Then hast thou drunk the heavenly dew ;

  Then have thy feet in rapture trod

  The pathway of a thought of God ;

And death can show thee nothing new.

For heaven and beauty are the same,—

  Of God the all-informing thought,

  To sweet, supreme expression wrought,

And syllabled by sound and flame.

The light that beams from childhood's eyes,

    The charm that dwells in summer woods,

    The holy influence that broods

O'er all things under twilight skies,—

The music of the simple notes

    That rise from happy human homes,

    The joy in life of all that roams

Upon the earth, and all that floats,

Proclaim that heaven's sweet providence

    Enwraps the homely earth in whole,

    And finds the secret of the soul

Through channels subtler than the sense.

O soul of mine! Throw wide thy door,

    And cleanse thy paths from doubt and sin;

    And the bright flood shall enter in

And give thee heaven for evermore!

WORDS.

THE robin repeats his two musical words,
   The meadow-lark whistles his one refrain ; /
   And steadily, over and over again,
The same song swells from a hundred birds.

Bobolink, chickadee, blackbird and jay,
   Thrasher and woodpecker, cuckoo and wren,
   Each sings its word, or its phrase, and then
It has nothing further to sing or to say.

Into that word, or that sweet little phrase,
   All there may be of its life must crowd ;
   And lulling and liquid, or hoarse and loud,
It breathes out its burden of joy and praise.

A little child sits in his father's door,
   Chatting and singing with careless tongue;
   A thousand beautiful words are sung,
And he holds unuttered a thousand more.

Words measure power; and they measure thine;
   Greater art thou in thy prattling moods
   Than all the singers of all the woods;
They are brutes only, but thou art divine.

Words measure destiny. Power to declare
   Infinite ranges of passion and thought
   Holds with the infinite only its lot,—
Is of eternity only the heir.

Words measure life, and they measure its joy!
   Thou hast more joy in thy childish years
   Than the birds of a hundred tuneful spheres,
So—sing with the beautiful birds, my boy!

SLEEPING AND DREAMING.

I SOFTLY sink into the bath of sleep :
  With eyelids shut, I see around me close
The mottled, violet vapors of the deep,
  That wraps me in repose.

I float all night in the ethereal sea
  That drowns my pain and weariness in balm,
Careless of where its currents carry me,
  Or settle into calm.

That which the ear can hear is silent all ;
  But, in the lower stillness which I reach,
Soft whispers call me, like the distant fall
  Of waves upon the beach.

Now like the mother who with patient care
   Has soothed to rest her faint, o'erwearied boy,
My spirit leaves the couch, and seeks the air
   For freedom and for joy.

Drunk up like vapors by the morning sun
   The past and future rise and disappear;
And times and spaces gather home, and run
   Into a common sphere.

My youth is round me, and the silent tomb
   Has burst to set its fairest prisoner free,
And I await her in the dewy gloom
   Of the old trysting tree.

I mark the flutter of her snowy dress,
   ` I hear the tripping of her fairy feet,
And now, pressed closely in a pure caress,
   With ardent joy we meet.

I tell again the story of my love,
   I drink again her lip's delicious wine,
And, while the same old stars look down above,
   Her eyes look up to mine.

I dream that I am dreaming, and I start;
   Then dream that nought so real comes in dreams;
Then kiss again to reassure my heart
   That she is what she seems.

Our steps tend homeward. Lingering at the gate,
   I breathe, and breathe again, my fond good-night.
She shuts the cruel door, and still I wait
   To watch her window-light.

I see the shadow of her dainty head,
   On curtains that I pray her hand may stir,
Till all is dark; and then I seek my bed
   To dream I dream of her.

Like the swift moon that slides from cloud to cloud,
  With only hurried space to smile between,
I pierce the phantoms that around me crowd,
  And glide from scene to scene.

I clasp warm hands that long have lain in dust,
  I hear sweet voices that have long been still,
And earth and sea give up their hallowed trust
  In answer to my will.

And now, high-gazing toward the starry dome,
  I see three airy forms come floating down—
The long-lost angels of my early home—
  My night of joy to crown.

They pause above, beyond my eager reach,
  With arms enwreathed and forms of heavenly grace;
And smiling back the love that smiles from each,
  I see them, face to face.

They breathe no language, but their holy eyes
　　Beam an embodied blessing on my heart,
That warm within my trustful bosom lies,
　　And never will depart.

I drink the effluence, till through all my soul
　　I feel a flood of peaceful rapture flow,
That swells to joy at last, and bursts control,
　　And I awake ; but lo !

With eyelids shut, I hold the vision fast,
　　And still detain it by my ardent prayer,
Till faint and fainter grown, it fades at last
　　Into the silent air.

My God ! I thank Thee for the bath of sleep,
　　That wraps in balm my weary heart and brain,
And drowns within its waters still and deep
　　My sorrow and my pain.

I thank Thee for my dreams, which loose the bond
   That binds my spirit to its daily load,
And give it angel wings, to fly beyond
   Its slumber-bound abode.

I thank Thee for these glimpses of the clime
   That lies beyond the boundaries of sense,
Where I shall wash away the stains of time
   In floods of recompense :—

Where, when this body sleeps to wake no more,
   My soul shall rise to everlasting dreams,
And find unreal all it saw before
   And real all that seems.

OLD AND BLIND.

GALLANT Gray-beard, can't you see
  You unconscionable bat, you—
While you play the devotee,
  That the girl is laughing at you?

You were handsome in your day,
  You are well preserved and thrifty,
And your manners, one may say,
  Are superb, but—you are fifty!

Don't be foolish, now you're old,
  Flirting in this feeble fashion,
Trying on a hearth grown cold
  To re-light a boyish passion.

7

You have had your day of youth,

   With its tender freaks and fancies;

You have known a woman's truth,

   And have lived Love's sweet romances.

Ay, I know her lips are red;

   True, her curls are black and glossy;

Yes, she bears a dainty head,

   And her eyes are sweet and saucy.

But she knows you act a part,

   While you try to tease and please her,—

Knows, Old Make-Believe, your heart

   Is as dead as Julius Cæsar;—

Knows it, though a simple girl,

   And is laughing while you linger;—

Knows it well, and, like a curl,

   Winds you round her jewelled finger!

But if you must act a part;

   If you cannot drop your feigning,

Feign you have not in your heart

   Such a thing as love remaining.

Come and stand with me, my friend,—

   She'll permit you—never doubt her!

Do as I do, and pretend

   Not to care a fig about her!

HER ARGUMENT.

" DONALD'S dead," she murmured, smiling, as she

   met me at the door.

  " Come and see the little fellow ere we carry him

    away ! "

Then she turned with queenly gesture, and walked

   firmly on before,

  To the chamber where the coffin and its lovely

    burden lay.

She was not of earth that morning ; she was up

   among the spheres—

  Cloud and darkness underneath, and round her

    paradisal air—

For her eyes had seen a vision that forbade their
falling tears,

And her heart had framed an argument that banished her despair.

Smiling lips and waxen forehead, folded hands and
pulseless breast,

There he lay—the household treasure—to be hid-
den ere the night!

And the mother stood above him with her hands together pressed

In a rapture of thanksgiving—in a transport of delight!

Then she spoke: " An angel met him at the parting
of his breath,

For he reached his hands up swiftly, and he answered with a smile!

Ah my Donald, darling Donald! Thou art conqueror
 of death!
 Evil cannot now disturb thee, nor the touch of sin
  defile.

" Do not stray too far, my Donald! Linger for me
 on the hills !
 Oh, there's time enough for straying! Wait and
  see it all with me!
I shall go to thee when graciously the Heavenly
 Father wills,
 And I know that I shall know thee, whensoever it
  may be !"

I had come to bring her comfort, but I stood in
 dumb amaze,
 For her peace was like a river and her joy too full
  for speech.

I had come to lead her sobbing through the dim and
doubtful ways

That philosophy discloses and the hackneyed school-
men teach.

She had learned a better logic; she was mistress of
the hour;

And I stood before her, humbled, knowing that my
scheme was vain.

" Tell me, woman," said I, trembling—" tell me, if
thou hast the power,

How thou knowest that this little boy of thine shall
live again? "

" Sweetest thing in earth and heaven "—made she answer to my quest—

" Life of Godhead, breath of angels, every good
and gift above,

Was bestowed upon my Donald—lived and throbbed

    within his breast—

God had given him love for largess, and had given

    him power to love !

"If He had not loved my Donald, would He, think

    you, have bestowed

What was best in all His kingdom—what was royal

    and divine—

On the little earthly nature, till I knew it the

    abode

Of the presence of The Master, and revered it as

    a shrine ?

"God is bountiful, but gives not gifts like this to

    stocks and stones !

His are all the living creatures on a thousand

    happy hills ;

But He only gives them pleasure, and a place to hide
their bones
When decay descends upon them, or the cruel
hand that kills.

" Would He fit a soul to love Him, and give nothing
in return?
Would He care a soul should love Him if He did
not love it well?
Love must find a love that answers, or with hopeless
passion learn ;
And God loves us, or our love is but the mockery
of hell.

" This is certain as the sunlight, this is true as life
is true :
And no soul can frame conception of a being so
inane,

7*

That, with power to save, He wills not to recover
and renew

Every object of His tenderness that falls in mortal
pain !

" Oh I know it : God loved Donald ; and He will not
let him die.

Even I had saved him living if my love had had
the might.

Did the God of earth and heaven love my darling
less than I ?

Having loved him will He damn him to the everlasting night ?

" That is not the way of loving. Every instinct of
love's power

Moves to shield its precious object from destruction
and decay ;

And I know that God loved Donald, and that Donald
has for dower

Immortality of being, in the everlasting day ! "

A LEGEND OF LEAP YEAR.

"No poet should invent his own romance." — *Stedman.*

" *One, two,*

Buckle my shoe."

Two little shoes with silver buckles dight,

Lay in the room where she had passed the night.

She raised them in her fingers, pink and white,

And put them on her feet, and strapped them tight.

" *Three, four,*

Open the door."

Then slowly rising from her cushioned chair,

She gave a last deft crinkle to her hair,

And oped the door and hurried down the stair—

Her petticoats soft rustling through the air!

" *Five, six,*

Pick up sticks."

Straight to the yard she skipped on queenly toes,

To where in serried ranks the wood-pile rose,

Then piled her arm with hickory to her nose,

And bore it to the house through air that froze.

" *Seven, eight,*

Lay 'em straight."

At length the wood was blazing on the fire,

Though still unequal to her fierce desire ;

And so she punched and punched the cheerful pyre,

And heaped with sticks the household altar higher.

" *Nine, ten,*

Good fat hen."

And then the eager hunger-fiend was foiled,

And she was glad, indeed, that she had toiled ;

For when her hands were washed, so sadly soiled,

She sat down to a last year's chicken—BROILED !

" *Eleven, twelve,*

Toil and delve."

Then to her waist her pink of pinafores

She fastened, and did up her little chores,

Made soap, made bread, baked beans, and swept her

floors,

And worried through a hundred household bores.

" *Thirteen, fourteen,*

Girls are courtin'."

Next morn before her door the grocer's van

Drove up. 'Twas leap-year, and she laid her plan.

So when he asked for orders, she began

To blush, and said she'd take a market-man !

" *Fifteen, sixteen,*

Girls are fixin'."

She overhauled her linen-chest with pride,

Bought hose, bought gloves, **bought** sheetings two

yards wide,

Bought blankets and a hundred things beside
That woman buys when she becomes a bride.

> " *Seventeen, eighteen,*
>
> *Girls are waitin'.*"

And then she waited—waited day by day,
Till weeks had flown, and months had passed away,
But still her order lingered in delay,
Although she longed to have it filled—and pay.

> " *Nineteen, twenty,*
>
> *Girls are plenty.*"

At length she knew. *Embarras de richesses*
Had thrown the fellow into wild distress,
And he had gone to drinking to excess,
Crushed by the weight of offered loveliness.

She called and saw him, selling by the pound
Within his stall. " Fact is," said he, " I found
That gals this year so wonderful abound,
No single market·man won't go around ! "

FALSE AND TRUE.

THE false is fairer than the true. Behold
Yon cloudy giant on the hills supine !—
The figure of a falsehood that doth shine,
Armored and helmeted, in such a gold
As in the marts was never bought or sold,—
Giant and armor the exalted sign
Of shapes less glorious and tints less fine—
Of forms of truth outmatched a thousand fold !
Ah, Poesie ! Thou charmer and thou cheat !
Painting for eyes that fill with happy tears,
In tints delusive, pictures that repeat
Dull, earthly forms in heavenly atmospheres !
How dost thou shame the truth, till it appears
Less lovely far than thy divine deceit !

THRENODY.

OH, sweet are the scents and songs of spring,
  And brave are the summer flowers;
And chill are the autumn winds, that bring
  The winter's lingering hours.
And the world goes round and round,
  And the sun sinks into the sea;
And whether I'm on or under the ground,
  The world cares little for me.

The hawk sails over the sunny hill;
  The brook trolls on in the shade;
But the friends I have lost lie cold and still
  Where their stricken forms were laid.

And the world goes round and round,

   And the sun slides into the sea ;

And whether I'm on or under the ground,

   The world cares little for me.

O life, why art thou so bright and boon !

   O breath, why art thou so sweet !

O friends, how can ye forget so soon

   The loved ones who lie at your feet !

But the world goes round and round,

   And the sun drops into the sea,   '

And whether I'm on or under the ground,

   The world cares little for me.

The ways of men are busy and bright ;

   The eye of woman is kind :

It is sweet for the eyes to behold the light,

   But the dying and dead are blind.

And the world goes round and round,
   And the sun falls into the sea,
And whether I'm on or under the ground,
   The world cares little for me.

But if life awake, and will never cease
   On the future's distant shore,
And the rose of love and the lily of peace
   Shall bloom there for evermore,
Let the world go round and round,
   And the sun sink into the sea!
For whether I'm on or under the ground,
   Oh, what will it matter to me?

TO MY DOG "BLANCO."

My dear, dumb friend, low lying there,
A willing vassal at my feet,
Glad partner of my home and fare,
My shadow in the street,

I look into your great brown eyes,
Where love and loyal homage shine,
And wonder where the difference lies
Between your soul and mine!

For all of good that I have found
Within myself or human kind,
Hath royally informed and crowned
Your gentle heart and mind.

I scan the whole broad earth around
For that one heart which, leal and true,
Bears friendship without end or bound,
And find the prize in you.

I trust you as I trust the stars;
Nor cruel loss, nor scoff of pride,
Nor beggary, nor dungeon-bars,
Can move you from my side!

As patient under injury
As any Christian saint of old,
As gentle as a lamb with me,
But with your brothers bold;

More playful than a frolic boy,
More watchful than a sentinel,
By day and night your constant joy
To guard and please me well,

I clasp your head upon my breast—
The while you whine and lick my hand—
And thus our friendship is confessed,
And thus we understand!

Ah, Blanco! did I worship God
As truly as you worship me,
Or follow where my Master trod
With your humility,

Did I sit fondly at His feet,
As you, dear Blanco, sit at mine,
And watch Him with a love as sweet,
My life would grow divine!

TWO HOMÈS.

I HASTEN homeward, through the gathering night,

Tow'rd the dear ones who in expectance sweet

Await the coming of my weary feet,

With faces in the hearth-fire glowing bright,

And please my heart with many a lovely sight

Of way-worn neighbors, stepping from the street

Through doors thrown wide, and bursts of light that

 greet

Their entrance, painting all their paths with white;

And then I think, with a great thrill of bliss,

That all the world, and all of life it brings,

Tell me true tales of other realms than this,

As faithful types of spiritual things;

And so I know that home's rewarding kiss

Insures the hope of heaven that in me springs.